THANKS A TON!

STORY BY SABRINA MOYLE   PICTURES BY EUNICE MOYLE

ABRAMS APPLESEED · NEW YORK

This is just a note to say
that I'm so grateful for the way
you helped me out the other day!

Finding grateful words is tough.
Sometimes I can't say enough!
So how about some

GRATEFUL STUFF?

Like how about this
TERRAPIN
for that time
you let me win?

And for that time you shared your room,

I hope you'll like this

BIG BABOON!

You cheered me up when I was blue,

so here's a
SILLY COCKATOO!

And how about this

CROCODILE...

for that time you made me smile?

You hugged me when
my day was hard,
so you deserve this

SAINT
BERNARD!

And here's a tub of
CHIMPANZEES

for all those times that you said,

"PLEASE!"

Your thoughtfulness made me go "WOW!" so here's a

HOLY MOLY COW!

You always have nice things to say. I hope this HIPPO makes your day!

And how about this large

RHINO?

(Because you're patient
when I'm slow.)

SLOW
AND
STEADY!

You gave up your seat on the bus.

YAY!

Please accept this **HUGE** WALRUS!

Remember that time you shared your lunch?

I sure do, so thanks a BUNCH!

Forget your kindness? Wouldn't dare!
So here's some super

UNDERWEAR!

I think you'll love
the ones with dots.
They mean,

THANKS AN AWFUL LOT!

For that time you held the elevator,

Remember when you helped me up?
Here's a massive TROPHY CUP!

made a huge difference . . .

To Eliane Ripka
—S.M.

To Bénédicte Brand
—E.M.

The illustrations in this book were created digitally.

Library of Congress Control Number 2019951467
ISBN 978-1-4197-4334-4

Text and illustrations copyright © 2020 Hello!Lucky
Book design by Hana Anouk Nakamura

Printed and bound in China
10 9 8 7 6 5 4 3 2 1

For bulk discount inquiries, contact specialsales@abramsbooks.com.

ABRAMS The Art of Books
195 Broadway, New York, NY 10007
abramsbooks.com